Tomi

Tomi Ungerer

Flix

TomiCO

AN IMPRINT OF

ROBERTS RINEHART PUBLISHERS

BOULDER · DUBLIN · LONDON · SYDNEY

For George Nicholson

Tomi Co

Published in the United States and Canada by
TomiCo
The Roberts Rinehart Publishing Group
6309 Monarch Park Place
Niwot, Colorado 80503

Distributed to the trade by Publishers Group West

Published in Ireland by
TomiCo
Town House and Country House Publishers
Trinity House, Charleston Road
Ranelagh, Dublin 6

Published in Great Britain by
TomiCo
Airlift Book Company
8 the Arena, Mollison Avenue, Enfield,
Middlesex, EN3 7NJ England

Published in Australia and New Zealand by
TomiCo
Peribo PTY Ltd.
58 Beaumont Road
Mount Kuring - GAI
NSW 2080 Australia

Jacket and interior illustrations © 1998 by
Diogenes Verlag AG Zürich

English translation © 1998 by
Roberts Rinehart Publishers

International Standard Book Number 1-57098-161-2

Library of Congress Cataloging-in-Publication Data
Ungerer, Tomi, 1931–
    Flix / Tomi Ungerer.
        p.   cm.
    Summary: Flix, a dog born to cat parents, finds
himself able to exist in two cultures, marries a cat,
and campaigns for mutual respect between cats and dogs.
    ISBN 1-57098-161-2
    [1. Dogs—Fiction.   2. Cats—Fiction.]   I. Title.
PZ7.U43F1 1998
[Fic]—dc21
                                        97-48298
                                        CIP
                                        AC

Manufactured in Belgium

10 9 8 7 6 5 4 3 2 1

Mr. Zeno Krall was a happy cat.
He was well off, he loved his wife Colza,
and they were healthy.
He was even happier when she announced,
"Darjeeling, I am expecting!"
"A visitor?"
"Yes, our child."
Mr. Krall, of course, was hoping for a boy.

When Mrs. Colza Krall, profusely bulging,
was seized by contractions, her caring husband
drove her to the hospital.
There he waited impatiently for the results.
All went well in the delivery room.
But nobody was ready to expect the unexpected—
Mr. Krall was beside himself when they told him,
"It's a boy—but . . . ."

When he found out that the boy was a dog(!)
he collapsed in a state of confusion.
At last he was given permission to visit his wife.
He showered her with flowers and kisses.
Then they looked at the baby.
It had a flat wrinkled face, drooping chops, and bulging eyes.
"How can it be—" he said. "What shall we do?"
"Love him. He is ours," replied Mrs. Krall.

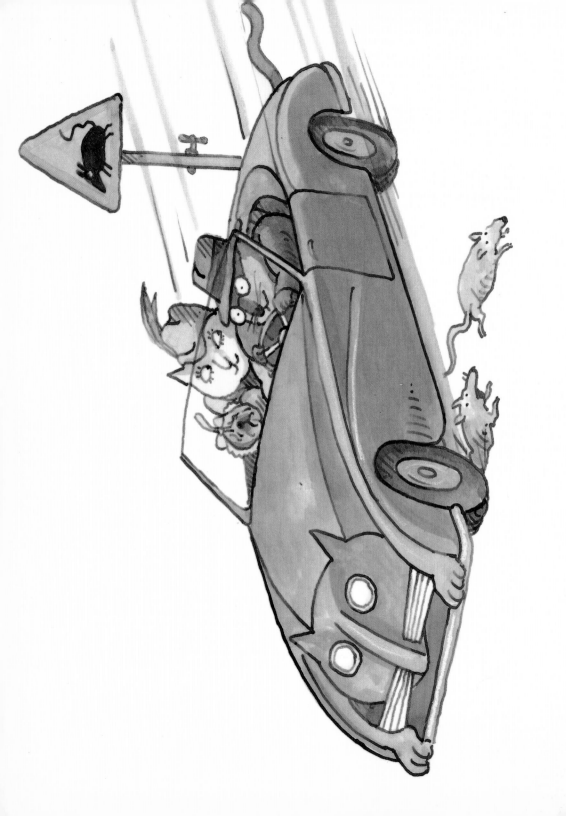

Mrs. Colza Krall recovered quickly.

After two days she was allowed to leave the hospital.

Mr. Krall fetched her in his catmobile.

"What will the neighbors say?" worried Mrs. Krall.

Facts are facts. They will get used to having a dog in their midst!"

The news created quite a stir.
In an interview, Mr. Krall explained:
years ago his grandmother was reputed
to have been secretly married to a pug,
and now, generations later . . .
here was the result!!!
"It is a genetic mishap!
And a very happy one for us," concluded Zeno Krall.

DOG BORN TO CAT PARENTS

WHAT NOW? GENES AMOK

A huge crowd of curiosity seekers gathered on the day of the baptism.

The baby pug was named "Flix."

The Kralls chose Dr. Medor Klops, a basset friend from Dog City, to be his godfather.

Flix grew up
good humored, bright, and kind.
From his parents he learned to speak cat,
which he uttered with a dog accent.
His mother filed his nails and taught him to climb trees.
Flix enjoyed his meals—
whether of fried mice, pickled canaries, or hot dogs—
and purred when Mommy Colza scratched him to sleep.

He spent a lot of time with his godfather, Uncle Medor,
who taught him to speak dog,
which he spoke with a slight cattish accent!
(In those days, dogs spoke dog, and cats spoke cat.
They could understand each other's language yet could not speak it.)
On weekends they all met,
and had picnics by the river.
Uncle Medor gave Flix swimming lessons.

And so Flix grew up,
inventing his own games,
for he had no friends
to play with.

Time came for him to enter school.
So . . . Mr. and Mrs. Krall decided
that Flix should go to dog school and
stay during the week with his uncle Medor.
After Flix had moved into his godfather's house,
Uncle Medor took him on a sightseeing tour.
They first strolled down Lassie Avenue,
which led to Laika Square.
"There," explained Uncle Medor,
"You see this monument?
It was erected in the memory of Laika,
the first dog ever to orbit in space."

Then they visited other neighborhoods,
like the eastern quarter thriving with Pekinese,
Chows, Afghans, Sharpeis, lit at night with paper lanterns.
"It is just the same in Cattown," said Flix. "We have the Siamese,
Burmese, Persians, Tonkinese, and they use the same paper
lanterns and wear the same clothes!"

Flix entered Pluto High School.
He was one of the smaller dogs in his class.
He soon made himself popular
with his quick wit and good disposition.
He was at the top of his class.

Musically talented, he learned to play
the violin, normally a cat's instrument.
He joined the local philharmonic orchestra.

Flix came home to his parents on weekends.
One Sunday morning, as they were strolling
along the river (on the cat side),
they heard calls for help.
Flix ran in the direction of the commotion.

A cat was fishing and
had caught a huge pike.
But the line got tangled around his body,
he was pulled in, and now . . . .
he was drowning!

Cats don't swim—dogs do, and Flix did.
He jumped in and rescued
the sinking cat,
dragging him back to shore,
and the pike as well.
With his parents, he had the pike for dinner.

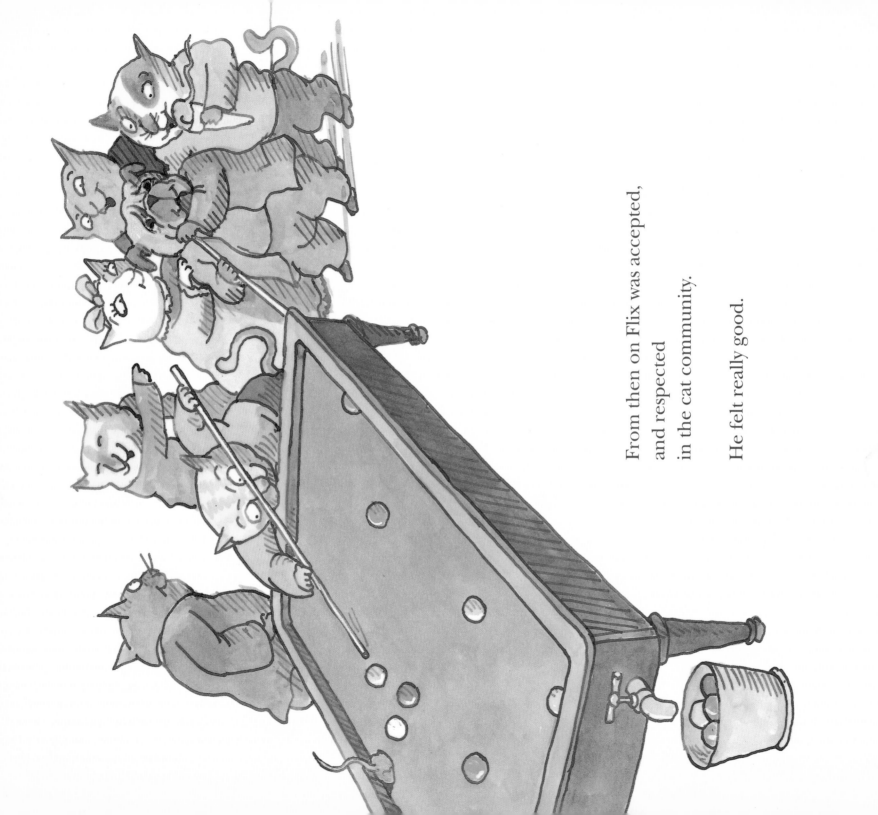

From then on Flix was accepted,
and respected
in the cat community.

He felt really good.

He finished school with honors and entered the university.
One day, as he was jogging through the campus
to clear his mind with exercise,
he heard screams for help.
A fire had broken out in the girls' dormitory.
From the fifth floor,
out of a window billowing with smoke,
a sophomore was crying for HELP.

Next to the building stood a dogwood tree.
Flix climbed the tree (like a cat)
to reach the branch nearest the window.
"Jump! I'll catch you. Now, right now!" he shouted.
She had NO choice.
She took the leap . . . and . . .

Flix caught her just in time.
The savior brought down the singed victim unhurt.
She recovered her senses
and they introduced themselves to each other.
Her name was Mirzah de la Fourrière,
a French exchange student.

She and Flix met, and met, and met again.
They became inseparable because . . .
they were in love, deeply IN LOVE.
They took walks in the moonlight,
had dinners by candlelight and, in short,
were delighted with each other.

When Flix introduced his fiancée to his parents, Mister and Madame Krall took an instant liking to their future daughter-in-law. Thrilled, they decided to celebrate the engagement immediately at the Eldorado, a posh restaurant in Cattown (that night the restaurant owner made an exception for the cat-sized canine).

NO DOG HERE

They married after Flix's and Mirzah's graduation.
The wedding was a huge affair,
drawing crowds from both sides of the river.
The nuptial march was performed for the first time
by a mixed choir of cats and dogs.
Faces were flooded with tears on both sides of the aisle.

When they returned from their honeymoon
Flix and Mirzah moved into a home of their own.
Flix entered his father's mouse and rat trap business,
expanding it by selling traps
in Dog City—collecting the baited proceeds
and selling them to butcher shops in Cattown.

Flix went into politics—
his deeds and personality had made him
very popular on both sides of the river.
He created a new party, the CDU—Cats and Dogs United.
He campaigned for a joint administration
of the two cities, mixed education, shared language,
mutual respect, and equal rights.
The day he was elected the first-ever Lord Mayor of
both towns, his wife Mirzah, née de la Fourrière,
announced she was with child.

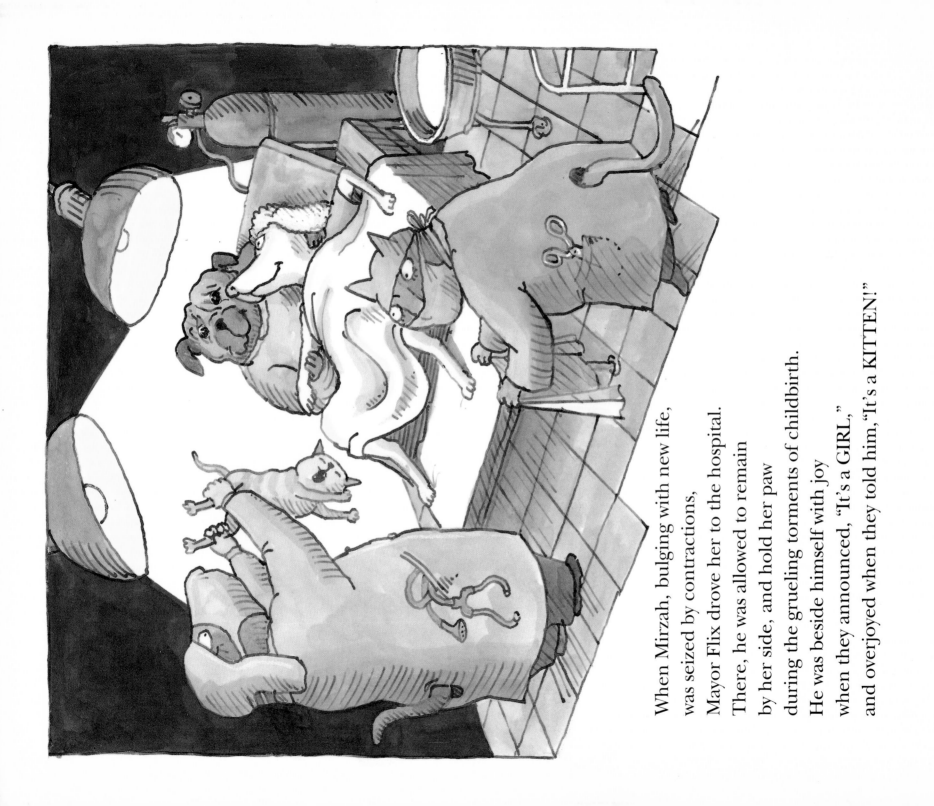

When Mirzah, bulging with new life,
was seized by contractions,
Mayor Flix drove her to the hospital.
There, he was allowed to remain
by her side, and hold her paw
during the grueling torments of childbirth.
He was beside himself with joy
when they announced, "It's a GIRL,"
and overjoyed when they told him, "It's a KITTEN!"